Dear Parents and Educators,

Welcome to Penguin Young Readers! As parents and educators, you know that each child develops at his or her own pace—in terms of speech, critical thinking, and, of course, reading. Penguin Young Readers recognizes this fact. As a result, each Penguin Young Readers book is assigned a traditional easy-to-read level (1–4) as well as a Guided Reading Level (A–P). Both of these systems will help you choose the right book for your child. Please refer to the back of each book for specific leveling information. Penguin Young Readers features esteemed authors and illustrators, stories about favorite characters, fascinating nonfiction, and more!

The Loopy Coop Hens Snow Hens	MAR 2017	LEVEL **2** GUIDED READING LEVEL **I**

This book is perfect for a **Progressing Reader** who:
- can figure out unknown words by using picture and context clues;
- can recognize beginning, middle, and ending sounds;
- can make and confirm predictions about what will happen in the text; and
- can distinguish between fiction and nonfiction.

Here are some **activities** you can do during and after reading this book:
- Picture Clues: Use the pictures to tell the story. Have the child go through the book, retelling the story just by looking at the pictures.
- Problem/Solution: The problem in the story is that all the hens want to make the beak for their snow hen. Discuss the solution in the story and how all the hens have a chance to be creative!

Remember, sharing the love of reading with a child is the best gift you can give!

—Sarah Fabiny, Editorial Director
 Penguin Young Readers program

*Penguin Young Readers are leveled by independent reviewers applying the standards developed by Irene Fountas and Gay Su Pinnell in *Matching Books to Readers: Using Leveled Books in Guided Reading*, Heinemann, 1999.

For Hailey—JMS

PENGUIN YOUNG READERS
An Imprint of Penguin Random House LLC

Copyright © 2016 by Janet Morgan Stoeke. All rights reserved. Published by Penguin Young Readers,
an imprint of Penguin Random House LLC, 345 Hudson Street, New York, New York 10014.
Manufactured in China.

Library of Congress Cataloging-in-Publication Data is available.

ISBN 9780448488431 (pbk)   10 9 8 7 6 5 4 3 2 1
ISBN 9780448488448 (hc)   10 9 8 7 6 5 4 3 2 1

⇒ The Loopy Coop Hens ⇐

Snow Hens

by Janet Morgan Stoeke

Penguin Young Readers
An Imprint of Penguin Random House

Snow

It is snowing at

Loopy Coop Farm.

Midge and Pip and Dot

love the snow.

They are making a snow hen.

"You make the tail, Midge,"
says Pip.

"I'll make the beak."

"Can I make the beak?"

asks Dot.

"I like beaks."

"The beak has to be just right, Dot.

This beak has to say, I am a beak!"

"Pip, the beak
will not talk.
It is just snow,"
says Midge.

"No, Midge!

It is ART!

Art must SING!"

"You will see," says Pip.

"THIS beak will make it sing."

"That beak will make it

YOUR snow hen,"

says Midge.

"We all want to make

the beak, Pip."

"I think I will make

something else," says Dot.

"Fine," says Pip.

"I am going to make

something else, too.

I am going to make a snow fox."

"A FOX!

Why?

We don't like foxes!" says Midge.

Midge wonders if Pip is crazy.

The Snow Fox

"This fox will be art," says Pip.

"And Rooster Sam will love it."

"Rooster Sam likes snow hens,"

says Midge.

"Well, maybe he will like

this better," says Pip.

"Everyone likes hens

more than foxes,"

says Midge.

She pats her hen.

Then Pip pats her fox.

"Oh!" says Pip.

"The ear fell off!

You!

You made me pat him!"

"I did not!" says Midge.

"I only patted my hen.

Your fox ear looks like a beak!"

"Well, your beak looks like a fox ear," says Pip.

17

"Oh NO!" says Midge.

"Don't, Pip!

Our ART!"

Pip is mad.

"It IS a fox ear!"

she says.

19

"Oh no," says Pip.

"This is not art."

"Not anymore," says Midge.

"Do you think we can

make them again?"

"Let's try," says Pip.

And they do.

More Snow

"Now we can give them both to Rooster Sam," says Midge. "Where is Rooster Sam?" wonders Pip.

"I don't know," says Midge.

"I can't see Dot, either."

"Dot!" they call.

"Oh dear," says Midge.

"She is so hard to see

in the snow," says Pip.

"Dot! Dot!"

"Here I am!" says Dot.

"I made something

for you and Pip.

Come and see!"

"Ta-da!" says Dot.

"It's Rooster Sam!"

say Midge and Pip.

"For US?

Oh, Dot!

It is wonderful!"

says Midge.

"You are so good, Dot," says Pip.

"This really is art."

Pip is a little bit sad.

"Yes, but look, Pip!" says Midge.

"We can be art, too!"

"We look like snow hens,"
says Dot.

"And we sing!" says Midge.

"Oh, Midge," says Pip.

"You are right!"

"We are the best art of all."